# The Burrowfolk Chronicles
## The Heart Oaks Whisper
By: B. Humphrey

This is a work of fiction. Names, characters, places, and incidents are the product of the author's imagination or used fictitiously. Any resemblance to actual persons, living or dead, or actual events is purely coincidental.

Dedicated to you:
May you always find a reason to smile

# A Whisper in the Wind

Hazel was the first to notice it—a scent, crisp and sweet, riding the breeze like a secret. It smelled of wet bark and woodsmoke, of honeycomb dripping in the sun, and moss freshly stirred by a curious paw. The forest air felt cool against her cheeks, carrying the sharp bite of autumn. Beneath it all, like a hidden thread in a tapestry, there was something else—a wild, earthy smell, as if the very roots of the forest were awake and whispering ancient stories.

Hazel Jacobs—"Hazy" to her friends—stood at the edge of a twisted old hawthorn tree, its branches tangled as if frozen mid-dance. Beside her, her younger brother Finnegan "Finn" Brightwood, freckled and restless, dragged the toe of his boot through the golden leaf-litter. The forest around them seemed to hum, a low and constant vibration just below hearing, as though it were alive and waiting for something.

The hawthorn stood like a sentinel at the heart of a little glade, where sunlight dripped through gaps in the branches, painting everything in dappled gold and shadow. Hazel knelt down to brush away a thick blanket of leaves—and there it was, nestled between the roots: a little wooden door, barely big enough for a rabbit to slip through.

It was painted a weathered shade of green, with tiny cracks along the edges. A brass keyhole glimmered faintly, as if kissed by moonlight, and carved above the arch of the door were three delicate symbols—an oak leaf, a mushroom, and a star. Hazel ran her fingers over the carvings, feeling the slight give of the wood beneath her touch, as if the tree itself were breathing.

Finn crouched beside her, his wide green eyes glittering with excitement. "Do you think it leads anywhere?" he whispered, his voice hushed as if the forest were listening.

Without waiting for her answer, Finn pressed his small hands against the door and gave it a gentle nudge. It swung open silently, as if it had been waiting for someone to find it. Beyond the threshold, a soft glow flickered—not the harsh light of lamps or flashlights, but the warm, buttery glow of candlelight. It spilled out onto the roots like melted gold.

Hazel glanced at Finn. He was already slipping through the little door, his grin wide with mischief. "Come on, Hazy," he whispered. "What's the worst that could happen?" With a sigh that was half-amusement, half-resignation, Hazel crawled in after him.

The world beyond the door was a wonderland, folded beneath the skin of the earth. The air was warm, scented with fresh-baked bread, lavender, and the faint tang of fermented honey. The earthen walls of the tunnels curved gently like the inside of a seashell, smooth and cool beneath Hazel's fingertips, yet dusted with soft moss that tickled her skin.

Acorn lanterns hung from twisted root hooks, casting little pools of light that swayed and danced as if alive. Tiny, clear bells—no bigger than thimbles—jingled whenever the warm air stirred, their sound like drops of water falling into a still pond.

The ground beneath their feet was packed firm with earth, scattered with round stones that gleamed like river pebbles. Along the edges of the tunnel, patches of soft lichen glowed faintly, as if absorbing the light from the lanterns and whispering it back into the dark.

Finn reached out to touch a lichen patch, giggling as it twinkled under his fingers. "It feels like fur," he said, grinning at Hazel.

Suddenly, from behind a corner, there came a shuffle and a snuffle, followed by the soft tap of tiny feet. A creature emerged, small and quick as a breeze—a mouse wearing a vest of violet velvet, its whiskers twitching curiously beneath a pair of gold-rimmed spectacles.

"Greetings, travelers!" squeaked the mouse in a voice that was bright and brisk, like a sprig of mint. He gave a low, polite bow, whiskers nearly brushing the floor. "I am Ember Quickpaw, scribe of the Burrowlands. And you've arrived just in time!"

"In time for what?" Finn asked, tilting his head.

"For the curse, of course," Ember replied, as if it were the most obvious thing in the world. "But let's not stand here in the draft! Come along, quickly now—there's a warm hearth waiting just around the bend."

Ember scurried ahead, his little feet pattering against the stone. The siblings followed, the tunnel widening until it opened into a burrow room, cozy and glowing with firelight. Hazel inhaled deeply—the air was thick with the scent of cinnamon, clove, and the buttery richness of spiced bread baking in the oven.

The room was filled with creatures of all shapes and sizes—rabbits with tiny aprons tied around their waists, squirrels knitting scarves from rainbow-colored yarn, and moles carefully carving wooden toys by candlelight. A plump rabbit, fur as white as snow and dusted with flour, bustled over to them with a tray of steaming mugs.

"Ah, new faces! Welcome, welcome! I'm Marigold Softpaw, herbalist and baker at your service," she said, her voice warm and buttery. She handed them each a mug, the contents shimmering like liquid sunlight.

Hazel took a cautious sip—it tasted like warm honey, apples kissed by frost, and just a hint of lavender. It left a pleasant warmth blooming in her chest, as if she had swallowed a summer afternoon.

Beside the hearth, a badger with grizzled fur and twinkling eyes stirred a bubbling pot that smelled of spiced cider. His wide paws moved with practiced ease, and the room filled with the comforting sound of wooden spoons scraping against iron.

"Come sit, come sit!" the badger called, waving a large wooden ladle. "I'm Tumble Brewburrow, master of ales and tales! Any friends of Ember are friends of mine." He gave a hearty chuckle, his laugh rolling through the room like the rumble of distant thunder.

The siblings found seats near the hearth, feeling the warmth of the fire seep into their bones. Finn leaned close to Hazel, his eyes wide with excitement. "This place is amazing, Hazy," he whispered.

"It really is," Hazel murmured, brushing crumbs from her lap as she nibbled on a piece of berry tart. The crust was flaky, the filling sweet and tart in perfect measure, bursting with the flavor of autumn berries freshly picked from enchanted brambles.

Just as Hazel began to feel she might never want to leave this cozy little world, the atmosphere shifted. The soft hum of conversation dimmed, and the creatures began glancing nervously at one another, their ears twitching and tails flicking.

Ember cleared his throat and adjusted his spectacles. "I suppose it's time to tell you why we're all gathered," he said, his whiskers twitching with unease. "You see, something's gone wrong with the Heart Oak Tree, the very source of all the magic in the Burrowlands. Its roots have begun to wither, and if the Heart Oak dies..."

He didn't need to finish the sentence. Hazel could feel the weight of his words in the stillness that followed, as heavy as damp earth on a rainy day.

Marigold wrung her flour-dusted paws anxiously. "We've never seen anything like it before," she whispered. "It's as if a shadow has fallen over the roots, and it's spreading faster than we can stop it."

Tumble gave a solemn nod, his usually jolly face dark with worry. "And when the Heart Oak falters, so does all the magic we hold dear. No more light in our lanterns, no more herbs to soothe restless dreams..." He trailed off, stirring the pot absentmindedly.

Hazel glanced at Finn, her heart thudding in her chest. The magic of this world was unraveling, and they had stumbled into it just as the first threads began to fray.

Before Hazel could ask what they were supposed to do, Ember's whiskers twitched with sudden resolve. "There's still hope," he said, his voice firm. "We'll need brave souls to venture deeper—beneath the Heart Oak's roots, to where the magic still sleeps. If we can awaken it, the curse may yet be broken."

Finn's eyes sparkled with excitement. "We'll help," he blurted out, before Hazel could stop him. Marigold smiled warmly. "Brave little ones," she said. "We'll need all the help we can get."

And just like that, Hazel and Finn found themselves at the beginning of an adventure woven from light and shadow, acorns and embers—an adventure that would take them through enchanted gardens, beneath ancient roots, and into the heart of the Burrowlands' deepest magic.

The wooden door behind them had closed quietly, unnoticed, and Hazel felt in her bones that there would be no turning back

**Not that she would want to.**

# 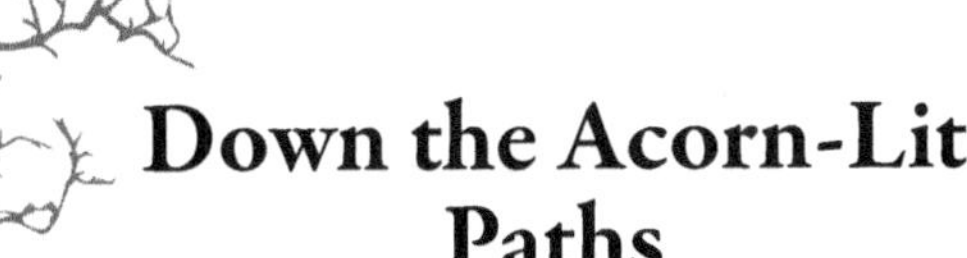 Down the Acorn-Lit Paths

The tunnel seemed to breathe as Hazel and Finn walked deeper, the soft **whisper of roots shifting overhead** filling the air like a lullaby. The earth beneath their feet was cool and comforting, sprinkled with smooth stones that glimmered like **polished moonstones**. The moss lining the walls gave underfoot with a pleasant squish, releasing a subtle scent of **petrichor and chamomile**.

Every few steps, the siblings passed tiny niches carved into the walls, each filled with **odd trinkets and treasures**: glass acorns, feathers with glowing tips, and tiny hand-carved animals that seemed to shift positions when no one was looking. It felt like the burrow itself was alive, full of secrets it was happy to share—if you were clever enough to catch them.

"Keep close," squeaked Ember Quickpaw as he scurried ahead, his little tail twitching with each step. "The paths twist and tangle like threads on an old loom. One wrong turn and you could end up lost for days—maybe weeks." Finn grinned. "What happens if you get lost down here?" he asked, skipping over a shiny pebble.

Ember glanced over his shoulder, adjusting his gold-rimmed spectacles with a tiny paw. "Oh, well," he said, with a cheerful shrug, "the **mole folk** might take you in. They're Lovely creatures, but terrible conversationalists, they only talk about dirt."

As if summoned by mention of their name, a small **mole with soot-covered paws** shuffled out from a side tunnel, dragging a lantern on a string. "Hullo there," the mole said in a low, gravelly voice. "Name's **Molewort Diggle**, at your service." He tipped his tiny felt hat. "Need any directions? Or perhaps a lantern upgrade?"

"We're just passing through, Molewort," Ember replied with a polite nod. "These two are heading to the village." The mole gave them a friendly sniff and shuffled back into the shadows, muttering to himself about "soil quality" and the "proper balance of clay to loam." His lantern glowed with a steady blue light, casting eerie but friendly shadows that danced along the walls.

The tunnel widened as they reached the heart of the burrow network, and Hazel gasped at the sight before her. The village stretched out like a little city woven beneath the roots of an ancient oak. **Round burrow doors**, each painted a different color, peeked from alcoves along the walls, while **mushroom houses** with soft, glowing windows clustered together like family gatherings.

Tiny **streams trickled** through the village, crossing under arched bridges made of braided twigs. Squirrels zipped along tightropes strung between branches, while **rabbits** in aprons bustled between burrow doors, carrying baskets filled with **fresh herbs** and **jars of golden honey**. A group of **mice musicians** sat on an overturned log, playing lively tunes on fiddles no larger than a leaf.

"Welcome to the Heartward Village," Ember said proudly, his whiskers twitching with excitement. "It's always festival season somewhere down here."

The scent of **baking bread** and **spiced cider** wafted through the air, mingling with the earthy aroma of moss and mushrooms. Every corner of the village seemed alive with music, laughter, and the soft rustling of leaves carried on a breeze that had somehow found its way underground.

"Come on!" Finn tugged at Hazel's sleeve, eager to explore. They wandered through the winding streets, passing **market stalls** where creatures sold enchanted wares. A squirrel offered **scarves woven with protective charms**, while a mole sold jars of **morning dew** collected from rose petals.

Finn stopped at a stall where a **fox** with fiery fur and bright, clever eyes was playing a tune on a silver flute. "Hello there," the fox said with a grin. "Name's **Foxglove Nimblefoot.** Fancy a song for the road?"

Before they could respond, Foxglove launched into a lilting melody that seemed to **dance through the air,** carrying with it the feeling of sunlight on your skin and the sound of autumn leaves crunching underfoot.

As they explored deeper into the village, Hazel noticed that the soft hum from earlier—like a song with no beginning or end—was growing louder. It came from the center of the village, where the earth gave way to a wide, open chamber. **Roots twisted up from the ground**, forming arches that cradled the air like cathedral rafters. And in the center of it all stood the **Heart Oak Tree.**

The Heart Oak was unlike anything Hazel had ever seen. Its **bark shimmered** with streaks of silver, as though the moon had laid its fingers upon the wood. Its roots spread outward in spiraling patterns, curling around stones and winding through the burrow walls. Even the leaves, though golden with autumn's touch, seemed to pulse with a quiet, ancient magic.

"Every burrow begins and ends with the Heart Oak," Ember whispered reverently. "It's the source of our light, our magic, our songs... and our dreams."

But as Hazel looked closer, she saw something troubling. One of the great **roots**—a root as thick as a barrel—was dark and withered, curling inward like a hand grasping for air. **Cracks spread** through the bark, and the shimmer that clung to its surface had dulled, like a star losing its light.

Finn knelt beside the root, brushing his fingers over the cracked bark. "What's happening to it?" he asked, his voice hushed.

"It's the curse," came a voice from behind them. Hazel turned to see **Marigold Softpaw**, the herbalist rabbit, standing with a basket of dried flowers in her paws. Her warm smile was still there, but a shadow of worry flickered in her bright eyes. "It's spreading faster than we feared."

As the children stood beneath the roots of the Heart Oak, a deep sense of purpose settled over Hazel, as though the very soil beneath her feet were calling out to her. She knew, without being told, that their arrival in the Burrowlands was no accident.

Ember Quickpaw cleared his throat, adjusting his spectacles once more. "We'll need brave hearts to journey beneath the deepest roots," he said, "to where the magic still lingers. It won't be easy—shadows have taken hold down there, and not all creatures that walk in shadow are friendly."

Marigold gave a solemn nod. "There's an old passage beneath the tree—a path few have dared take in years. If you can reach the heart of the roots, you might be able to **wake the magic** before it's lost forever."

Tumble Brewburrow, the badger, waddled forward, offering them each a **small bottle filled with glowing amber liquid**. "A sip of this will keep your courage warm," he said with a wink. "But don't drink it all at once—it's strong stuff."

Hazel glanced at Finn, her heart thudding in her chest. This was no ordinary adventure—they were being asked to step into a world that felt both wondrous and dangerous, as if the magic itself teetered on the edge of a dream.

Finn grinned, excitement dancing in his eyes. "We're ready," he said confidently, clutching the bottle of amber liquid.

Hazel wasn't sure she shared her brother's boldness, but something deep inside her—something ancient and quiet—told her that this was exactly where they needed to be.

As the creatures of the Burrowlands looked on with hopeful eyes, Ember gave them a small, encouraging smile. "Then let's not waste another moment," he said. "The path to the roots waits for no one."

And with that, the siblings stepped forward, ready to follow the winding paths that led beneath the Heart Oak—into the very heart of the Burrowlands' magic.

# The Heart Oak's
# Secret

The path to the Heart Oak wound deeper into the earth, and with each step, the **air grew cooler**, thick with the scent of **loamy soil, old bark, and distant rain**. Tiny fireflies floated lazily overhead, their light pulsing in time with the soft hum that ran beneath Hazel's feet, as if the tree's magic were breathing—**a slow, steady rhythm** that wove through the ground like a heartbeat.

"Stay close," Ember Quickpaw whispered, his whiskers twitching nervously. "The roots don't always welcome visitors this far down." Finn, undeterred, gave Hazel a grin. "I bet the tree knows we're coming to help."

Hazel nodded, though her heart fluttered with a mix of excitement and unease. Something about the **hum beneath the earth** felt off-kilter, like a familiar song sung out of tune.

They pressed onward, the tunnel narrowing until it opened suddenly into a vast chamber—and there it was, **the Heart Oak**, standing tall and ancient, its roots curling like rivers frozen in mid-flow.

The tree's bark shimmered faintly with streaks of silver and gold, as though it had absorbed the **light of every season** it had seen. **Its roots spread outward**, burrowing through the earth like veins, curling into arches and alcoves that cradled the soft hum of life. Even the leaves, though touched with the first kiss of autumn, still shimmered with a quiet, hidden magic.

At the base of the tree stood **Elder Thistle**, a tortoise as old as the roots themselves. His shell was worn and moss-covered, his eyes the color of amber and deep with centuries of stories. **Tiny mushrooms sprouted along the ridges of his shell**, glowing faintly as he looked up at Hazel and Finn with a gaze that was both patient and knowing.

"You've come," Elder Thistle said, his voice slow and deliberate, as though each word had traveled through time to reach them. "The Heart Oak has been waiting."

Hazel and Finn approached the ancient tree, and Elder Thistle gestured toward the roots. "Place your hands here," he murmured. "The Heart Oak will show you what it knows."

Without hesitation, Hazel pressed her palms against the cool bark, and Finn did the same beside her. The moment their hands touched the tree, **a wave of warmth** rushed through them—**a golden light blooming behind their eyes**, pulling them into a vision that felt both distant and familiar.

In the vision, they saw **autumn sprites dancing**, their wings glowing like flickering embers. The sprites spun in spirals around the Heart Oak, **weaving threads of light through the roots**. Their laughter was the sound of wind through dry leaves, and their joy spread like wildfire—**but something dark hovered at the edges.**

From the shadows stepped a figure cloaked in twilight—a **sorceress**, her eyes gleaming like cold iron. She whispered words in a forgotten language, weaving **dark magic into the roots**, and the light that once flowed through the Heart Oak began to dim.

**Leaves withered and fell**, and the sprites' wings drooped, their glow flickering like dying embers.

The vision shifted, and Hazel saw the **Heart Oak's roots twist in pain**, curling inward as if trying to protect themselves from the creeping shadow. A voice—low and ancient—whispered through the vision: **"The curse feeds on fear... and doubt... and time..."**

The vision shattered, and Hazel gasped as she was pulled back into the present. The air around her felt heavier, as though the **weight of the vision** had settled into her bones. Finn blinked, his face pale. "Did you see it too?" Hazel nodded, her heart thudding in her chest. "The sorceress... she tried to steal the magic from the Heart Oak."

Elder Thistle gave a solemn nod. "Long ago, the sorceress sought to bind the tree's power for herself, but the magic resisted her. She was cast out, but a fragment of her curse remained—**a seed of darkness** hidden deep within the roots. Now that curse has begun to awaken, and it grows stronger with every flicker of doubt it finds." Finn crouched by the roots, running his fingers over the bark's fine cracks. "How do we stop it?" he asked.

"The magic of the Heart Oak is bound to the seasons," Elder Thistle explained. "And the curse weakens it by feeding on fear. To heal the tree, you must restore **hope and trust**—in yourselves and in those around you."

Hazel felt the weight of the task settle over her like a heavy cloak. The vision had shown her how deeply the curse had woven itself into the roots—**it was no ordinary shadow.** If they were to save the tree, they would need more than courage. They would need **wisdom, kindness, and belief in the magic that still lingered beneath the soil.**

Elder Thistle leaned closer, his amber eyes gleaming. "You must also speak with **Bramble the Owl**, at the Clock Tower Elm. He knows more about the sorceress than anyone left in the Burrowlands."

As Hazel and Finn prepared to leave, the **roots of the Heart Oak shifted**, parting just enough to reveal a small **acorn pendant** hidden among them. The pendant shimmered with a soft silver light, and when Hazel touched it, she felt a faint hum of magic run through her fingers.

"The Heart Oak offers this gift," Elder Thistle murmured. "It is a token of trust—for your courage, and for the journey ahead." Finn grinned, slipping the pendant into his pocket. "We won't let the tree down," he promised.

Hazel smiled, though the hum of the vision still echoed in her heart. The path before them was clear—but it would not be easy. As they left the chamber, the distant hum of the Heart Oak followed them, vibrating gently beneath their feet. The magic of the Burrowlands was still alive—**but the curse was growing, and time was running short.**

"Come on, Hazy," Finn whispered, nudging her with a grin. "Let's go find that owl." With lanterns glowing softly and the weight of the pendant warm in her hand, Hazel felt ready for whatever lay ahead. The magic of the Burrowlands was waiting—**and so were the answers hidden beneath the roots.**

# The Clock Tower Elm and the Owl's Warning

The path wound deeper, quieter than before, and with every step, Hazel and Finn felt as if the tunnels were holding their breath, waiting for something. The walls, once lively with firefly light and the hum of burrowfolk life, grew dim, their glow fading into a cool silver that clung to the air like morning mist. The scent of wet stone and cedar drifted around them, mingling with the faint spice of dried leaves.

Marigold's soft paws pattered beside them, and Ember Quickpaw darted ahead, lantern swinging from his small claws. "Not far now!" he squeaked over his shoulder. "We'll be at the Clock Tower Elm before the next bell!"

Finn leaned toward Hazel, grinning. "Do you think the owl will be big?"

Hazel glanced down at the feather charm that dangled from her fingers, still warm from where Bramble had tucked it into her hand in the vision beneath the Heart Oak. "I bet he's ancient," she whispered. "And very, very wise."

The idea of meeting a creature with centuries of stories settled over her like the first snowfall of winter—both thrilling and just a little unnerving.

The tunnel opened suddenly into a grand, circular chamber. At its heart stood the Clock Tower Elm, a tree so large it seemed to hold the weight of the entire forest above. Its gnarled trunk twisted upward, disappearing into the shadows, and perched high in its branches was a great brass clock, its hands ticking slowly and deliberately. The air around the tree shimmered with age, as if every moment lived here just a little longer than it should.

The clock's pendulum swung like a heartbeat, ticking with the steady patience of the seasons. Its soft chime echoed through the chamber, carrying with it the scent of frost-touched leaves and woodsmoke, as though the tree remembered every autumn it had ever seen.

Hazel stepped forward, her boots brushing against roots that curled like ancient rivers, worn smooth by the passage of time. She tilted her head, catching sight of a glimmer of feathers among the shadows.

Then, with a rustle as soft as the wind through dry leaves, Bramble the Owl appeared.

Bramble swooped down from the elm's highest branches, landing gracefully on a low root. His feathers shimmered like autumn frost, flecked with gold and copper, and his large amber eyes glinted with quiet understanding. Wisdom sat on his wings like dust, gathered from a thousand forgotten stories.

"Ah," Bramble murmured, tilting his head slowly as his gaze swept over Hazel and Finn. "So the wind has carried you here at last." His voice was deep and deliberate, like the tolling of a distant bell.

Finn's eyes widened. "You knew we were coming?"

The owl gave a slow blink. "The Heart Oak's roots whispered your arrival long before your feet touched the burrows. They carry the stories of everything that lives beneath them." His gaze lingered on Hazel, and she felt as though Bramble could see every thought, every doubt, and every hope she carried tucked inside her heart.

Bramble shifted his wings, settling himself on the root as if preparing to tell a tale that had waited too long to be spoken. "The curse you face is no simple spell," he began. "It is a shadow left behind by one who sought to bend the magic of the Heart Oak to her will."

"The sorceress," Hazel whispered, the memory of the vision flickering in her mind.

Bramble gave a solemn nod. "Long ago, she tried to steal the magic that flows through these roots, believing it could be hers alone. But magic, like time, belongs to no one—it is wild, and it resists captivity. When the sorceress failed, she cast a curse instead, planting a shadow deep within the Heart Oak. That shadow has grown quietly ever since, feeding on fear, on doubt, and on fractured trust."

Finn shivered beside Hazel, clutching his lantern closer. "How do we stop it?" The owl's amber eyes darkened. "The curse cannot be destroyed by force. It must be bound with light and hope—through magic that flows freely, not by command. And to do that, you must gather what is needed before the Festival of Embers."

The Festival of Embers and the Gathering of Herbs "The Festival of Embers?" Finn echoed, curiosity lighting his face. Bramble ruffled his feathers, and his voice took on the rhythm of an ancient rhyme, as though he spoke the memory of the seasons themselves:

"Under lantern's glow and moonlight bright,
With song and flame, we chase the night.
The Heart Oak stirs where the embers fall,
But without trust, the light will stall."

The owl's gaze sharpened. "To prepare for the festival, you must gather enchanted herbs—yarrow, moonflower, and dreamroot. Each carries a magic the Heart Oak needs to heal."

Marigold's ears twitched nervously. "We'll have to collect them from the Garden of Lullabies," she murmured. "That's no easy task."

Finn's grin spread wide. "A garden that sings? This is going to be amazing!" Hazel, however, noticed the flicker of caution in Marigold's eyes. "What's the catch?" she asked quietly.

Bramble's feathers rustled as though in warning. "The curse is clever. It will not sit idle while you gather what is needed. It will twist the garden's song, turning hope into doubt. You must hold fast to each other, for the shadows will try to lead you astray."

Before they could leave, Bramble extended one wing toward Hazel, producing a small bundle wrapped in soft bark. Inside lay seven silver threads, each as thin as a whisper, glowing faintly in the lantern light.

"These threads," Bramble murmured, "will bind your lanterns together, ensuring their light does not falter. No matter how dark the path becomes, you will find each other through the glow of these threads."

Hazel tucked the bundle carefully into her pocket, her heart steady beneath the weight of the owl's gift. "Thank you," she whispered.

Bramble gave a slow nod. "May the light guide you and the shadows falter."

With the owl's warning lingering in their minds, Hazel, Finn, and Marigold made their way back through the twisting tunnels. The hum of the Heart Oak followed them, steady but fragile, like a song waiting for its chorus.

Ember scurried ahead, lantern swinging merrily despite the seriousness of their mission. "To the Garden of Lullabies, then!" he chirped. "We'll have those herbs in no time!"

Finn nudged Hazel with a grin. "See? We've got this, Hazy."

Hazel smiled back, though the memory of the sorceress's shadow still whispered at the edges of her thoughts. The road ahead would not be easy—but with light in their lanterns and hope in their hearts, she knew they would face whatever came.

As they disappeared deeper into the burrows, the threads of silver light tucked safely in Hazel's pocket, the soft ticking of the clock above echoed behind them—a reminder that time, like magic, waits for no one.

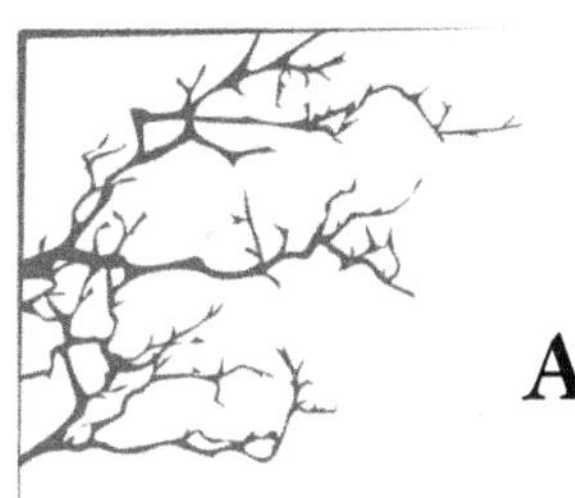

# A Garden of Lullabies

The path to the Garden of Lullabies was like **wandering through a dream**. The tunnels grew quieter, and the air began to smell of **lavender, wild mint, and moonlit water**, as if the soil itself exhaled the fragrance of night. **Moss glowed faintly beneath their feet**, and here and there, delicate silver roots dangled like chandeliers, draped with **threads of spider silk** that shimmered when touched by the faint light of their lanterns.

Ember Quickpaw led the way, his little nose twitching with excitement. "Not much farther now!" he whispered. "The garden hums louder under the stars—it sings, it does!"

Finn grinned. "This place keeps getting better."

Hazel wasn't so sure. There was a weight in the air now, **a tension that curled at the edges of her thoughts**, as if the curse was already stirring, waiting to test their resolve.

When they emerged from the tunnel, **the Garden of Lullabies stretched out before them like a world spun from moonlight.** Overhead, **a web of roots and branches** arched high, framing slivers of the night sky. **Starlight trickled through cracks in the earth,** splashing across the garden in puddles of silver. Everywhere Hazel looked, flowers swayed gently, their petals humming soft, lilting tunes that seemed to **melt into the air like lullabies.**

Along the edges of the garden, **moonflower vines curled and climbed**, their blossoms glowing in the dim light. **The dreamroot plants nestled among soft moss beds**, their leaves shimmering in shades of silver and green. Clusters of **yarrow flowers**, bright as tiny suns, bobbed gently, as if nodding to the rhythm of the garden's song.

The air here was thick with magic—**a soft, pulsing hum**, as if the plants were singing to one another in languages older than time. Each flower carried a note, and together, they wove a melody so delicate it felt like **the memory of a lullaby your heart had never forgotten.**

Finn knelt beside a patch of dreamroot, brushing his fingers over its leaves. "It feels... soft, but also sharp," he whispered.

"That's dreamroot for you," Marigold said softly. "It hums brighter when it knows it's needed."

They began to collect the herbs in **gentle, careful handfuls**. Marigold showed them how to pluck yarrow flowers without disturbing their roots, her paws light and precise. **Hazel gathered moonflower petals**, cradling them like precious treasures. The petals were cool against her fingers, humming softly as they fell into her hands.

Finn worked beside her, placing dreamroot leaves into Marigold's basket. "It smells like... like my room at Grandma's," he whispered, smiling. "But... better."

Hazel smiled too, though the quiet joy of the garden felt fragile, like **a candle flickering in a cold wind.**

Then, as they finished gathering the last of the yarrow, a sudden **shift in the air** stopped Hazel in her tracks. The garden's gentle melody faltered—**just for a moment, but enough to leave the air heavy with unease.**

From the far corner of the garden, **the shadows thickened**, and the hum of the plants turned strange—off-key, like a song being pulled apart thread by thread.

Hazel turned, and her breath caught in her throat. **There, among the moonflowers, stood a familiar figure**—a girl with Hazel's own face, but her eyes were cold and empty, and her smile was twisted into something that didn't belong.

"Go home, Hazel," the shadow said softly. "This place isn't yours to save."

Finn gasped, and Hazel saw another shape step out from the shadows—**a version of Finn, twisted and wrong**, with a sneer on his face. "You'll leave her behind," the shadow-Finn whispered. "Just like you always do."

**The melody of the garden shifted again**, turning eerie, the notes spiraling into strange, discordant patterns. The shadows pressed closer, whispering doubts and fears Hazel hadn't even known she carried.

Finn's face paled, and he looked to Hazel, confusion clouding his bright eyes. "Hazy... I wouldn't leave you," he whispered.

Hazel's heart clenched. The shadow was pulling them apart—**twisting their fears into something real**. She could feel the doubt curling inside her, cold and relentless, like ivy creeping through cracks in stone. Marigold's voice cut through the rising panic, sharp and urgent. "Don't listen! It's the curse—it feeds on fear."

Hazel gripped the **feather charm from Bramble** tightly, feeling the warmth of the owl's magic hum against her skin. She closed her eyes, forcing herself to focus—not on the twisted lies the shadows whispered, but on **Finn's hand still wrapped firmly around hers**.

"I trust you," Hazel whispered, her voice steady despite the fear knotting in her chest. "And I know you'd never leave me." Finn blinked, and the confusion in his eyes cleared. "Never," he whispered fiercely.

The shadows hissed, recoiling like mist burned by morning light. With **the shadows retreating**, Hazel raised the feather charm high, and its silver threads glowed brighter, casting soft beams of light across the garden. The notes of the lullabies slowly returned—soft and harmonious once more, **like a breeze weaving through autumn leaves**.

The twisted versions of Hazel and Finn melted away, slipping back into the dark soil from which they'd sprung. Marigold let out a soft sigh of relief. "You did it," she whispered, her ears twitching with joy.

The herbs around them **swayed gently**, as though singing their gratitude. The moonflower vines curled closer, their blossoms glowing brighter, and the dreamroot leaves unfurled, **humming contentedly**.

As they stood, catching their breath, a small flutter of wings stirred the air. From among the moonflowers appeared **tiny fae creatures**, their wings glittering like frost and their eyes gleaming with quiet mischief.

"You passed the test," one of the fae whispered, her voice like the sound of a distant bell. "The garden sings for you now." Another fae flitted forward, sprinkling **silver dust over their lanterns**. "May the light guide your path, and may the shadows falter in your presence."

The fae danced once more among the herbs, their laughter light as autumn breeze, before disappearing into the starlit branches above.

With the herbs safely gathered and the **garden singing behind them**, Hazel, Finn, Marigold, and Ember made their way back to the burrow. **The lanterns glowed softly**, their light steady and warm, the silver threads from Bramble ensuring their flame wouldn't falter.

Hazel held the feather charm close as they walked, feeling the quiet pulse of the Heart Oak's magic calling them forward. They had passed the garden's test, but she knew that **the hardest part of their journey still lay ahead.**

The Festival of Embers was waiting—and so was the final confrontation with the curse. Finn nudged her with a grin, his lantern swinging cheerfully at his side. "See, Hazy? We've got this."

Hazel smiled, though the weight of what lay ahead settled quietly in her chest. But as they disappeared into the winding tunnels, **the song of the garden lingered in the air**, bright and hopeful—a promise that the light would always find them, no matter how dark the path became.

# The Ale-Maker's Tale

The scent of **spiced honey and crackling wood** greeted Hazel, Finn, Marigold, and Ember as they stepped back into the warmth of **Tumble Brewburrow's cozy den**. The walls were lined with shelves cluttered with **bundles of dried herbs, stone mugs**, and **lanterns flickering with enchanted flames**. Tumble stood at the hearth, stirring a **large pot of bubbling amber-colored ale**, the steam curling lazily toward the ceiling like a contented sigh.

"There you are!" Tumble rumbled, his voice a warm growl, as he turned toward them. His **fur shimmered with silver streaks**, and the firelight danced in his cheerful, round eyes. "I was beginning to wonder if the shadows got the better of you." Finn grinned, sliding into a seat near the fire. "Almost, but we gave 'em a good scare."

"Ah, good!" Tumble chuckled, handing a mug of **honey-foam ale** to each of them. "This should take the chill off your bones."

Hazel wrapped her hands around the **stone mug**, the warmth of the ale spreading through her fingers. She took a careful sip—**the taste was like apple cider kissed by summer rain, with just a hint of winter's frost**. Finn downed his eagerly, foam clinging to his upper lip, and Marigold gave a soft laugh, her nose twitching in delight.

Once they had settled around the hearth, the den grew quiet. **Only the soft crackle of the fire and the gentle hum of magic in the air remained.** Tumble leaned back in his seat, his large paws cradling his mug, and gave a low sigh, the cheer in his eyes dimming slightly.

"You've seen it, haven't you?" he asked softly. "The curse." Hazel nodded, the memory of the **twisted shadows** still heavy in her heart. "We saw... versions of ourselves. Things we're afraid of."

Tumble grunted, nodding. "Aye. That's the way of it. The curse doesn't come with fangs and claws—it comes in the quiet, **through cracks of doubt and fear.** That's how it grows."

The badger leaned closer, his voice dropping into a storyteller's cadence, warm and deliberate. "You see, the sorceress wasn't always what she became. Once, she was a wanderer, someone with more magic in her heart than most knew what to do with. But she grew lonely—believed she could steal magic for herself, twist it into something permanent, something she could keep."

He stirred his mug absently, his gaze distant. "But magic doesn't work that way. **It isn't meant to be owned**—it's meant to be shared, to ebb and flow like the tides. When the Heart Oak refused her, she cursed it out of anger. She couldn't take the magic, so she poisoned it instead."

Finn leaned forward, eyes wide with curiosity. "But the curse—how is it still here? The sorceress is gone, isn't she?"

Tumble gave a grim smile. "Her body is long gone, lad, but a curse like hers doesn't just fade. It **lurks in the roots**, waiting for a chance to take hold. Every fear, every doubt—it feeds on that, grows stronger through it."

Hazel felt the weight of the badger's words settle deep in her chest. **The shadow they had faced in the garden was only the beginning.**

"And here's the most dangerous part," Tumble continued, his voice soft. "The curse doesn't always stay where it belongs. Sometimes... it finds a way to slip into someone's heart. **Anyone carrying enough anger, hurt, or fear can become its vessel.**"

Marigold shivered beside Hazel, her ears flattening against her head. "You mean... it could be inside someone already?" Tumble gave a slow nod. "Aye. And it's crafty—it'll hide where you least expect it."

Hazel exchanged a glance with Finn, her heart beating faster. **The curse could be closer than they thought—maybe even among the burrowfolk.** If they didn't act quickly, it could spread beyond the Heart Oak's roots, unraveling everything the burrowfolk had worked to protect.

"We need to finish the binding ritual," Hazel whispered. "Before the curse gets stronger." Tumble nodded solemnly. "The Festival of Embers will be your best chance. The magic of the festival will strengthen the Heart Oak—**but only if the burrowfolk believe in it again.**"

Finn frowned, his excitement dimming slightly. "What do you mean?"

"Hope is like fire," Tumble murmured. "It spreads when it's shared. But if there's doubt—**even a flicker—it can snuff out the light before it takes hold.** You'll need to unite the burrowfolk, get them to trust in the magic again. Without that, the ritual won't hold."

Hazel tightened her grip on the **feather charm**, the warmth of Bramble's magic thrumming beneath her fingers. She glanced at Finn, who gave her an encouraging smile, and then at Marigold, whose quiet strength steadied her nerves. "We can do it," Hazel whispered, more to herself than anyone else. "We have to."

Tumble gave a satisfied grunt, lifting his mug in a silent toast. "That's the spirit, lass. Now, let's make sure you have everything you need."

He reached into a wooden chest beside the hearth and pulled out **a small flask**, filled with a **pale golden liquid that sparkled faintly in the firelight**. "This here is an enchanted ale—just a drop will **boost the magic of your lanterns** and keep the shadows at bay."

He handed the flask to Hazel with a wink. "But be careful—**magic works best when used sparingly.** Too much, and it might do more harm than good."

With their **lanterns glowing brighter** and the flask tucked safely into Hazel's bag, the group prepared to leave Tumble's burrow. **The air outside felt colder**, as if the shadows had crept closer while they rested by the hearth. But the warmth of Tumble's words—and the strength of the **new-found hope in their hearts**—kept the chill at bay.

"Go on, then," Tumble rumbled, ushering them toward the tunnel entrance. "The Festival of Embers won't wait forever—and neither will the curse."

Ember scampered ahead, his lantern swinging happily. "We'll light the brightest lanterns the burrows have ever seen!" he declared, his whiskers twitching with excitement.

Finn gave Hazel a playful nudge. "See? I told you we've got this."

Hazel smiled, though the weight of the task ahead still lingered quietly in the back of her mind. **The path to saving the Heart Oak was becoming clearer, but it wouldn't be easy.** There were still shadows waiting—**and doubt could creep in when least expected.**

As they walked through the winding tunnels, **the soft hum of the Heart Oak vibrated beneath their feet**, steady but fragile, like the pulse of a sleeping giant. The weight of the **feather charm in Hazel's hand felt reassuring**, a quiet reminder that they were not alone.

She glanced at Finn, who gave her a quick grin, and at Marigold, who walked beside them with quiet determination. **Whatever came next, they would face it together.**

"The festival will be beautiful," Marigold whispered, her voice full of quiet hope. "And when the Heart Oak blooms again... everything will feel right."

Hazel nodded, holding tightly to that hope as they disappeared into the dark, their lanterns glowing brighter with each step.

The Festival of Embers awaited—and so did the final test of the **sorceress's curse.**

# The Festival of Embers

The night of the **Festival of Embers** arrived like a whispered promise—**a sky brushed with twilight**, soft as the down of owl feathers, and the air fragrant with the scents of **autumn leaves, woodsmoke, and honeyed cider**. The burrowfolk gathered beneath the towering roots of the **Heart Oak**, lanterns in hand, as the hum of ancient magic vibrated through the ground, more fragile than ever.

Finn, Hazel, Marigold, and Ember stood at the heart of the gathering, their lanterns glowing with the **bright silver threads** Bramble had given them. Tiny **sprites with ember-like wings** flitted between the roots, their laughter sparkling like the first snowfall of winter. Around them, the burrowfolk hung **lanterns from low branches**, each one flickering with hope, waiting for the ceremony to begin.

Hazel breathed in the air, alive with excitement but tinged with uncertainty—**as though the forest was holding its breath, waiting to see if the magic would return.**

At the base of the Heart Oak, a great table had been set with offerings: **moonflower petals glowing like captured starlight**, sprigs of **yarrow tied with silver thread**, and vials of enchanted ale, each drop shimmering in the lantern light.

Finn nudged Hazel, his lantern swinging cheerfully at his side. "This is going to be amazing," he whispered. "We've got the herbs, we've got the lanterns—what could go wrong?"

But Hazel's heart tightened. She could feel the **shadows pressing at the edges of the celebration**, creeping through cracks in the roots like a cold wind. The curse wasn't gone—not yet. **It was waiting, watching.**

"Everyone needs to believe," she whispered back, gripping the **feather charm** tightly. "The magic won't work if they don't."

Marigold nodded solemnly. "Hope is the most fragile kind of magic—but it's the only one strong enough to save the tree."

As the sun disappeared below the horizon, the festival began. **Bramble the Owl** swooped down from the **Clock Tower Elm**, landing gracefully on a low branch of the Heart Oak. His amber eyes gleamed as he called out to the gathering.

"Tonight, we celebrate the light that lingers through every season," Bramble declared, his voice deep and steady. "We light these lanterns to honor the Heart Oak's magic, and to remind ourselves that even in the darkest nights, **hope is the brightest flame.**"

The burrowfolk cheered softly, lifting their lanterns high. **Each lantern flickered with a warm, golden light**, casting playful shadows across the roots. **Sprites danced in spirals**, their wings glowing like tiny embers, and **foxes played enchanted flutes**, filling the air with music that hummed through the roots like the pulse of the earth itself.

Finn grinned as he lit his lantern, the silver thread glowing brightly in his hand. "This is it, Hazy," he whispered. "This is where everything starts to feel right again."

Hazel smiled, though the flicker of doubt still curled in her chest. **They had gathered the herbs, prepared the magic—but the curse wouldn't let them succeed without a fight.**

As the first lanterns were hung from the Heart Oak's branches, the magic began to stir—**a soft glow spreading through the roots**, like embers catching flame. For a moment, everything felt perfect—the burrowfolk laughed and sang, and the Heart Oak seemed to hum in time with the celebration, as though **hope itself was starting to bloom.**

Then, without warning, a **cold wind swept through the gathering**, snuffing out the lanterns in a single breath. **The sprites' wings dimmed**, their glow flickering like dying stars, and the music faltered as the shadows beneath the roots deepened, twisting into shapes that slithered between the burrows.

Hazel gasped, clutching her lantern as the **shadows coiled closer**, whispering dark promises and old fears. "It's the curse!" she cried. "It's trying to stop us!"

Finn's lantern flickered dangerously, the silver thread trembling in his hand. "What do we do?" he whispered, fear flickering in his voice for the first time.

"The magic will only work if we believe in it," Marigold whispered urgently, her paws trembling as the shadows crept closer. "We have to light the lanterns again—together."

Hazel took a deep breath, forcing herself to focus—not on the cold press of the shadows, but on the warmth of **Finn's hand in hers** and the strength of **Marigold's quiet resolve**. "We can do this," she whispered, lifting her lantern high. "We just have to believe."

Finn nodded, his grip tightening around the silver thread. "I believe in us," he whispered fiercely. "We've made it this far—we're not stopping now."

Ember scampered onto a low branch, his tiny whiskers twitching with determination. "Light the lanterns!" he squeaked. "Before the shadows steal the night!"

With trembling hands, Hazel dipped the **yarrow sprigs** into the enchanted ale, whispering a quiet prayer beneath her breath. **The silver thread in her lantern glowed brighter**, and as she placed the lantern back on the Heart Oak's branch, a spark of light bloomed—small at first, but steady.

Finn followed suit, lighting his lantern with the moonflower petals they had gathered. The glow spread quickly, chasing the shadows back into the cracks of the roots. **One by one, the lanterns flickered back to life**, their light growing brighter and stronger with each flame.

The burrowfolk watched in awe as **the Heart Oak's roots began to stir**, curling upward like **tendrils of light weaving through the earth**. The hum beneath their feet grew louder, deeper—**a song older than memory**, welcoming the return of magic.

The shadows hissed, writhing as the light grew stronger. **They twisted and snapped**, but the lanterns burned too bright, fueled by the belief and hope of every creature gathered beneath the Heart Oak. The curse tried to cling to the edges of doubt, but there was no space left for it to hide.

As the lanterns flickered in unison, **the Heart Oak bloomed with light**—golden leaves unfurling, roots glowing like veins of starlight. The tree hummed with ancient magic, its song filling the air with a warmth that melted away every trace of the curse.

The burrowfolk cheered, their lanterns swinging high as the **sprites burst into joyful flight**, their wings trailing sparks through the night. **Music filled the air once more**, and the Heart Oak stood tall and proud, its roots winding deep into the earth, alive with renewed magic.

Bramble the Owl gave a low, contented hoot from his perch. "The light has returned," he murmured. "The Heart Oak's magic is yours again—if you keep it."

Hazel smiled, her heart lighter than it had been since they first stepped into the burrows. **The shadows were gone**, and the magic of the Heart Oak flowed freely once more.

As the festival continued beneath the glowing branches, Hazel and Finn stood side by side, their lanterns swinging gently in the breeze. "We did it," Finn whispered, his eyes bright with joy. "We really did it."

Hazel nodded, the warmth of the moment settling deep in her chest. **They had faced the curse, and they had won—together.**

Marigold beamed beside them, her whiskers twitching happily. "The Heart Oak is safe. The burrows are safe."

And as the celebration carried on, with music and laughter filling the night, Hazel knew that **the magic of the Heart Oak would always be with them**—a light that would never fade.

# Shadows Among Friends

The warmth of the **Festival of Embers** still lingered in the air as the burrowfolk returned to their homes beneath the roots of the Heart Oak. **Lanterns swayed gently in the tunnels,** their light casting soft, golden beams across the walls. The songs of the sprites echoed faintly, and for the first time in a long while, the Heart Oak's hum felt steady, as if it had awoken from a long, restless sleep.

But even as Hazel and Finn walked the winding paths back toward **Tumble Brewburrow's hearth,** something unsettled gnawed at the edges of Hazel's thoughts. **The curse was broken—so why did the shadows still feel so close?** The air carried a strange stillness, and Hazel couldn't shake the feeling that **something had been left unresolved.**

When they reached the village square the next morning, the unease Hazel had felt was mirrored in the burrowfolk. **Whispers drifted between market stalls,** and creatures that once greeted each other warmly now spoke in hushed tones, their eyes flickering with suspicion.

"The lanterns nearly went out last night," a mole muttered to his wife. "Someone must've brought the curse into the festival."

"Who can we trust?" a squirrel whispered to her friend. "What if the curse hasn't really gone?" Hazel felt her heart sink as she listened to the scattered conversations. **The shadows weren't just lurking in the dark anymore—they were stirring among the burrowfolk themselves.** Even with the Heart Oak's light restored, fear had taken root, **twisting trust into suspicion.**

Marigold stood beside Hazel, her ears drooping with worry. "They're scared," she whispered. "Fear lingers even after the curse is gone—it always does."

Finn's brow furrowed. "But we saved the tree. Why isn't that enough?" Ember Quickpaw scurried up onto Hazel's shoulder, his whiskers twitching. "It's the way of things," he said quietly. "Once doubt gets in, it's hard to shake."

As the day wore on, the tension in the village only grew. Creatures began to eye one another with mistrust, **their words sharp and unkind.** "You were acting strange at the festival," a squirrel accused a fox with narrowed eyes. "Maybe you're still carrying the curse!"

"I saw you leave before the lanterns went out," a mole grumbled at a hedgehog. "What were you doing in the shadows?" The air grew heavy with suspicion, and Hazel could feel the delicate peace they had fought so hard to restore begin to unravel. **If the burrowfolk couldn't trust each other, the magic of the Heart Oak would wither again.**

"We have to stop this," Hazel whispered to Finn, her voice tight with urgency. "The curse feeds on fear—if we don't stop it now, it'll take hold all over again."

The siblings gathered at **Tumble's burrow,** seeking the warm glow of the hearth and the comfort of familiar faces. Marigold sat cross-legged on the floor, sorting herbs from her basket, while Tumble stirred a **pot of sweet cider,** the steam curling like ribbons into the air.

"We need to remind everyone why they trusted each other in the first place," Hazel said, pacing the room as her thoughts churned. "Something that will bring them together."

Marigold's nose twitched thoughtfully. "A story?" she suggested. "Stories have power—they remind us of who we are." Finn perked up. "What about a storytelling contest? Like at the festival!"

Ember's whiskers quivered with excitement. "A contest judged by **Bramble!** That'll get everyone talking about the right things again—**not their fears, but their hopes.**"

Tumble gave a low rumble of approval. "A fine plan. **Stories are magic in their own way**—and maybe they're exactly what we need to banish the last of the shadows."

That evening, Hazel and Finn spread the word about the **storytelling contest**, and soon the village was abuzz with excitement. **The burrowfolk gathered beneath the Heart Oak** once more, lanterns swinging high, their faces lit with curiosity and anticipation.

Bramble perched on a low branch, his amber eyes gleaming as he surveyed the crowd. "Tonight, we share stories," the owl declared, his voice carrying through the roots like the toll of a distant bell. "Stories of light and shadow, of courage and fear. **The best story will win a feather from my wing—and with it, good fortune to carry forward.**"

One by one, the creatures came forward, weaving tales from their hearts. **The foxes told stories of winds that carried secrets**, and the moles spun tales of lanterns that glowed brighter when shared. Each story was different, but they all carried a spark of the same message: **Even in the darkest nights, the smallest light can make all the difference.**

When it was Hazel's turn, she stood before the gathering, her lantern glowing softly in her hand. **The words came easily, as though the story had been waiting inside her all along.**

"I've learned that the hardest magic to find isn't in herbs or lanterns or ancient trees," she began softly. "It's in trust. It's believing that even when things get dark, we can hold on to each other and find the light again."

Her voice wove through the crowd like a gentle breeze, and as she spoke, she could feel the weight of the **burrowfolk's fears begin to lift—like a mist evaporating beneath the first morning sun.**

When Hazel finished, the gathering fell quiet for a long, breathless moment. Then Bramble gave a slow, deliberate nod, his **amber eyes warm with approval.** "A fine story," he murmured. "And an important one."

He spread his wings, plucking a single feather from his side. **The feather shimmered like moonlight caught on water**, and as he handed it to Hazel, she felt its quiet magic settle into her heart.

The crowd erupted into soft cheers, and for the first time since the festival, Hazel felt the **last of the shadows slip away,** carried off by the joy and trust rekindled among the burrowfolk.

As the night wore on and the stories gave way to laughter and song, **the Heart Oak glowed brighter**, its roots curling deeper into the earth, alive with magic. **The burrows were whole again,** held together not just by magic, but by the simple, quiet strength of **hope and trust.**

Finn leaned close to Hazel, his lantern swinging gently at his side. "We did it, Hazy," he whispered, a grin spreading across his face. "For real this time."

Hazel smiled, her heart lighter than it had been in days. **The shadows were gone—but more importantly, the light had found its way back to the burrows.**

# Beneath the Stone Circle

The forest was quiet when Hazel, Finn, Marigold, and Ember reached the edge of the **ancient stone circle**. The moss-covered stones stood like **silent sentinels**, their surfaces cracked and weathered by centuries of wind and rain. **Twisted roots** curled around the stones, as if trying to pull them back into the earth, and the air felt heavy—thick with the weight of **old magic** and **forgotten promises**.

Hazel's lantern flickered in the gathering dusk, and she gripped the **feather charm from Bramble** tightly, feeling the steady hum of magic in its threads. **This was where the sorceress's magic had first taken root**, and the curse had lingered ever since, waiting for a chance to rise again.

Finn shivered beside her, wrapping his scarf tighter. "This place feels... wrong," he whispered. "Like it's been waiting for us."

"It has," Marigold murmured, her whiskers twitching anxiously. "This is where her power was cast—**and where it still lingers.**"

Ember scampered ahead, peering into the cracks between the stones. "The entrance is hidden beneath the roots," he squeaked, brushing aside the moss. "We have to go down—there's no other way."

Hazel knelt beside Ember, brushing her fingers over the moss. Beneath it, she found a **wooden trapdoor**, worn smooth by time. **Roots twisted across its surface**, as if trying to hold it shut, but with a little effort, Finn managed to pry the door open.

A wave of **cold, stale air** rushed up from below, carrying the scent of **damp stone and old parchment**. Hazel felt a shiver run down her spine, but she forced herself to breathe. **They had come too far to turn back now.**

With a soft click, she lit her lantern, and they descended into the darkness, **their footsteps echoing through the narrow tunnel** that spiraled downward into the heart of the earth.

The tunnel opened into a vast, circular chamber, where the walls were lined with **broken mirrors**—shards of glass that glimmered faintly in the lantern light, reflecting twisted versions of the world. At the center of the chamber stood a **stone altar**, cracked and worn, and beneath it, **the roots of the Heart Oak** curled like serpents, blackened and scarred by the curse that had taken hold so long ago.

Finn shuddered. "I don't like this," he whispered, his voice barely audible over the hum that vibrated through the air—**the sound of magic waiting to be unleashed.**

Marigold crouched beside the altar, brushing away dirt and debris. "This is where she cast her final spell," she murmured. "Her power was bound to the mirror shards—and they've been waiting ever since."

Ember's whiskers twitched nervously as he inspected the shards. "They're still dangerous," he whispered. "If we don't bind them properly, the curse could escape again."

As Hazel reached toward one of the larger shards, the glass shimmered—and suddenly, she saw **herself**, standing alone in a world where the Heart Oak had withered to dust. **The burrows were silent**, the lanterns extinguished, and her brother was nowhere to be found.

"No!" Hazel gasped, pulling her hand away, but the image clung to the edges of her mind, whispering that this was the future if she failed.

Finn stumbled back from another shard, his face pale. "I saw you, Hazy," he whispered. "You were gone. I couldn't find you."

**The mirror shards reflected their deepest fears**, twisting hope into doubt, casting shadows where there should have been light. The curse was clever—it would try to break them, **not with force, but with despair.**

"We have to stay together," Hazel whispered fiercely, gripping Finn's hand. "We can't let it trick us."

Marigold nodded, her expression determined. "We've already seen what fear can do. **We can't let it win this time.**"

With renewed focus, Hazel pulled the **obsidian pendant** from her pocket—the one they had found deep beneath the moat—and placed it at the center of the stone altar. **The symbols etched into the pendant glimmered faintly**, waiting for the magic to awaken.

Marigold spread the herbs they had gathered—**moonflower petals, yarrow, and dreamroot**—in a circle around the altar, while Ember lit seven tiny lanterns, placing them at equal intervals around the roots.

"We need to bind the shards with light," Marigold whispered. "And once the curse is trapped, we must **seal it with the pendant.**"

Hazel nodded, lifting her lantern high. "Let's do this."

Together, they began to speak the binding spell, their voices weaving through the air like threads of light:

**"By the roots that twist, by the leaves that fall,**
**By the moon's bright face and the lantern's call,**
**We bind this shadow, we seal this night,**
**Return to darkness—banished from light!"**

As the final words of the spell echoed through the chamber, the **mirror shards began to tremble**, their surfaces rippling like water disturbed by a stone. **The shadows within the glass hissed**, twisting and writhing, desperate to escape.

The roots beneath the altar curled upward, **grasping the shards** and pulling them into the heart of the circle. The shards shattered with a deafening crack, and for a moment, everything was silent—**too silent.**

Then, with a burst of dark energy, **the curse surged forward, a swirling mass of shadow and fury,** trying to break free from its prison. **The lanterns flickered wildly**, and the roots of the Heart Oak strained, struggling to hold the darkness in place.

"Now!" Marigold cried. "The pendant—place it at the center!" With trembling hands, Hazel grabbed the **obsidian pendant** and placed it on the altar. As soon as the pendant touched the cracked stone, **the binding symbols ignited**, glowing with brilliant silver light.

The shadows writhed one last time, **screaming as they were pulled into the pendant**, and then—**silence.** The curse was sealed, its magic bound within the obsidian, where it could no longer spread its darkness through the burrows.

The air in the chamber shifted—**lighter, cleaner, as if a great weight had lifted**. The roots of the Heart Oak pulsed softly with new life, and the lanterns burned bright and steady, their flames untroubled by the dark.

"We did it," Finn whispered, his eyes wide with disbelief. "It's over." Marigold gave a tired smile, brushing the dirt from her paws. "The Heart Oak will heal now," she murmured. "And so will the burrows."

Ember let out a triumphant squeak, his tiny paws clapping together. "I knew we could do it!"

Hazel smiled, though the exhaustion was beginning to settle into her bones. **They had faced the darkness—and won.**

With the curse sealed and the Heart Oak's magic beginning to flow once more, the group made their way back through the winding tunnels, **their lanterns glowing bright in the dark.**

As they reached the entrance to the village, they were greeted by the warm glow of lanterns and the sound of familiar voices—**the burrowfolk, waiting to welcome them home.**

Bramble the Owl watched from his perch, his amber eyes gleaming with quiet approval. "The light has returned," he whispered, spreading his wings in a gesture of blessing. "And so has the magic."

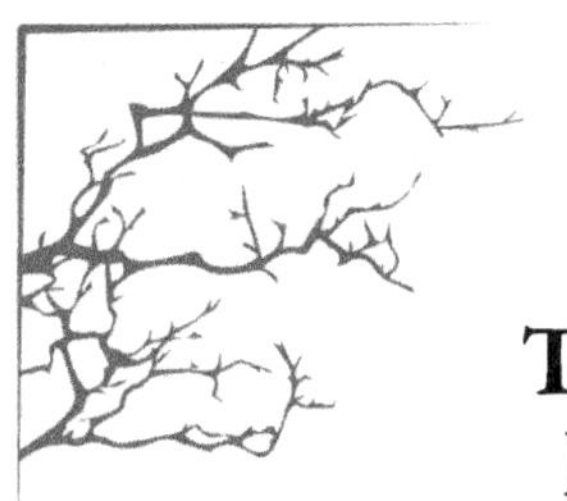

# The Mirror's Deception

The return to the village felt lighter, the lanterns warm and steady in their glow, but Hazel couldn't shake the strange **whisper tugging at the edges of her thoughts**. Even though they had sealed the curse within the obsidian pendant, there was something lingering—**a thread of magic left unresolved.**

When they reached Tumble Brewburrow's hearth that evening, the air was filled with relief. **The burrowfolk celebrated the victory** with mugs of enchanted cider, telling stories by the fire. But Hazel sat quietly, the warmth of the room unable to thaw the lingering cold knot in her chest. **Something wasn't right**—the mirror's reflections still flickered at the back of her mind, like a shadow waiting to be noticed.

Marigold noticed her unease and leaned closer, her whiskers twitching with concern. "What's on your mind, Hazel?" Hazel stared into the crackling fire, her hands wrapped tightly around the warm mug. "The curse is sealed, but... **why do I still feel like we missed something?**"

That night, Hazel woke with a start, the room dim and silent except for the soft crackle of the dying embers. **A whisper drifted through the darkness**, not from outside the burrow, but from inside her own thoughts.

*"The mirror holds more than shadows."*

She sat up, heart pounding, and reached for the feather charm still tucked beneath her pillow. The warmth of it steadied her, but the whisper remained—faint, persistent, like a memory just out of reach.

She knew what she had to do. **The mirror shards hadn't revealed everything.** There was still one truth hidden within them—a truth she had to uncover before it was too late.

At dawn, Hazel woke Finn and Marigold, explaining the lingering unease. Without hesitation, the three made their way back through the winding tunnels, **their lanterns glowing softly against the morning mist** that seeped into the burrows.

When they reached the **stone circle**, the air was still—**too still**, as if the earth beneath their feet was waiting for something to stir. The shards of the broken mirror still lay scattered across the chamber floor, glinting faintly in the dim light.

Hazel knelt beside the largest shard, her reflection twisting across its surface. But **this time, it wasn't fear she saw**—it was **herself**, standing beneath the Heart Oak, holding the obsidian pendant. And standing beside her was a **familiar figure cloaked in shadow**.

Finn's voice broke the silence. "What do you see, Hazy?"

She stared deeper into the shard, her heart thudding painfully in her chest. "It's the sorceress," she whispered. "She... she never left. **She's part of the mirror.**"

The reflection shimmered, and for a moment, Hazel saw the full truth: **The sorceress had not simply cursed the Heart Oak—she had bound herself to the mirror, hoping to one day return through it.** When the curse was sealed in the obsidian pendant, only part of her magic had been trapped. **A fragment**

**of her still lingered in the shards**, waiting for a chance to escape.

Marigold's eyes widened in horror. "If she's still in the mirror—" Hazel nodded grimly. "Then the curse isn't truly gone. **If we don't bind the mirror properly, she'll come back.**"

The shards began to shimmer, the twisted reflections within them stirring like a storm on the verge of breaking. **Dark whispers filled the chamber**, curling around them like smoke. The sorceress's voice echoed through the mirrors, sharp and cold.

"You think you can stop me?" she hissed. **"You've only delayed the inevitable."** The shadows in the shards twisted into familiar shapes—**Hazel's own reflection stared back at her**, smirking with cruel intent. Finn's reflection turned away, as though abandoning her to the darkness. Marigold's twisted form whispered of failure and regret.

But Hazel stood her ground, gripping the **feather charm tightly**. "You can't have this place," she said, her voice steady despite the fear creeping at the edges of her mind. **"Your power ends here."**

Marigold scattered **the last of the moonflower petals** around the shards, forming a perfect circle. Finn placed **the obsidian pendant** at the center, and Hazel knelt beside him, **her heart steady and her lantern burning bright.**

Together, they began to speak the binding spell, the words filling the chamber like the first light of dawn:

**"By moon and root, by flame and thread,**
**By lantern bright and words once said,**
**We bind the shadow, we seal the glass,**
**No more to stir, no more to pass."**

As the final words echoed through the chamber, the shards trembled violently, and **the sorceress's reflection twisted in fury. The shadows writhed**, trying to break free, but the circle of herbs and light held fast.

The obsidian pendant glowed with brilliant silver light, **pulling the remaining fragments of the sorceress's magic into itself**. The shards shattered with a sharp, final crack, and the whispers faded—**gone, at last.**

For a long moment, the chamber was silent, save for the steady hum of the Heart Oak's roots beneath their feet. Then, slowly, **the lanterns brightened**, their flames steady and strong.

"It's over," Hazel whispered, the words feeling lighter than air. **"Really over."**

Finn exhaled sharply "We did it," he whispered, a grin spreading across his face. "We actually did it."

Marigold smiled, her whiskers twitching with relief. "The Heart Oak is safe now. And so are the burrows."

Ember scampered onto Hazel's shoulder, his whiskers quivering with triumph. "I knew you could do it!" he squeaked. "A hero's story, through and through!"

As they left the chamber, the **first light of morning spilled through the forest**, illuminating the moss-covered stones with a soft, golden glow. **The air felt lighter**, the weight of the curse finally lifted, and the forest hummed with quiet magic—**the magic of life renewed.**

When they returned to the burrows, they were greeted by cheers and warm embraces. **The burrowfolk celebrated not just the victory, but the hope that had been restored.** The Heart Oak's leaves shimmered in the morning light, its roots stretching deep and strong, humming with the quiet promise of a new beginning.

Bramble watched from his perch in the Clock Tower Elm, his amber eyes gleaming with quiet pride. "You've done well," he hooted softly. "The magic is yours again—and so is the light."

Hazel smiled, her heart full as she stood beneath the branches of the Heart Oak. **They had faced the darkness—and they had found the light.**

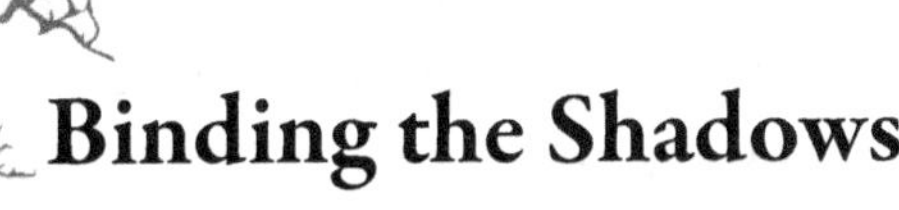

# Binding the Shadows

The burrowfolk gathered beneath the **Heart Oak's glowing branches**, their faces lifted toward the morning light that filtered gently through the leaves. **The curse was gone**, the sorceress's magic sealed, and the roots of the ancient tree thrummed with newfound strength—**a steady pulse of life, hope, and unity**. Yet, the memory of the shadows lingered like the last breath of a winter storm, urging them to ensure that fear would never take root in their hearts again.

Hazel, Finn, Marigold, and Ember stood quietly near the Heart Oak's trunk, lanterns still aglow, watching as the burrowfolk shared stories of the long night now safely behind them. **There was relief in every glance, every word**, but Hazel knew the light they had kindled would need to be nurtured to last.

Bramble, the ancient owl, fluttered down from the **Clock Tower Elm**, landing gracefully on a low branch. **His amber eyes glimmered with approval**, but there was still a note of caution in his gaze. "The shadows have been sealed," he said, his voice slow and deliberate, "but shadows have a way of returning if the light grows dim."

The gathered burrowfolk murmured in agreement, some shifting uneasily. They all knew the truth now: **magic was not**

**simply protection against fear—it required trust and unity to thrive.**

Tumble Brewburrow, the jovial badger, stepped forward with a warm grin, clutching **a large stone mug** brimming with enchanted ale. "So what do we do, eh?" he asked, raising his mug high. "What's the plan to keep those shadows where they belong?"

Hazel looked at her brother, and he gave her a small nod, as if to say, *this part is yours, Hazy.* She stepped toward the gathering, feeling the gentle hum of the **feather charm tucked into her pocket**, a reminder of the journey they had taken together.

"We make sure no one faces the shadows alone," Hazel said, her voice clear and steady. **"Fear grows in silence—but so does hope, if we let it.** We need to carry the light we found tonight with us, and share it with each other, no matter what."

The burrowfolk leaned in closer, listening. Finn grinned and added, "And we tell stories—lots of them! The best ones we've got. **Stories remind us who we are.** They remind us that the light's always there, even if we can't see it right away."

Bramble ruffled his feathers thoughtfully. "Then we must create a new tradition," he said. "A ritual to honor the magic we've rekindled, so the shadows never find their way back."

Tumble clapped his large paws together with a grin. "A lantern-lighting, every season! And a big ol' feast, too—something to bring everyone together."

Marigold nodded, her ears perking up. "And we could plant new herbs around the Heart Oak. **Yarrow for protection, moonflower for hope, dreamroot for strength.** We'll let them bloom as reminders that magic grows strongest when it's shared."

Ember scampered onto a nearby root, his whiskers twitching with excitement. "I'll write poems for it!" he squeaked. "One for each season—little rhymes to keep the shadows away."

The burrowfolk smiled, their faces bright with hope. **The shadows that had threatened to divide them would be held at bay—not through magic alone, but through the bonds they had forged.**

The group gathered beneath the Heart Oak's roots, where the **obsidian pendant** rested on the altar. The **binding spell had done its work**, trapping the sorceress's lingering magic within the black stone—but the burrowfolk knew that simply sealing the curse was not enough. **They had to bury it deep, out of reach, and let the earth itself protect the magic they had reclaimed.**

Together, they dug a small hollow beneath the Heart Oak's roots, where the pendant would rest. **Moonflower petals and yarrow sprigs** were scattered over the pendant, and Marigold sprinkled a few drops of enchanted ale over the ground, whispering a quiet blessing.

Bramble raised a wing, his voice deep and steady. "By the roots that cradle and the light that guides, we bind the shadows here, where they can do no harm. Let them sleep beneath the soil, and let the light above grow ever brighter."

Hazel and Finn knelt together, pressing their hands into the soft earth to cover the pendant. **The Heart Oak's roots curled gently around the spot**, sealing the magic deep within. **A soft hum spread through the ground**, not a warning this time, but a lullaby—a promise of peace.

With the pendant safely buried, the burrowfolk gathered around the Heart Oak for **the first of many lantern lightings.**

Each creature lit a lantern and hung it from the tree's low branches, where they swayed gently in the evening breeze. **The soft glow spread across the burrows**, casting a warm, steady light that chased away every lingering shadow.

Finn grinned as he hung his lantern beside Hazel's. "Think we'll get a story out of this adventure?" he asked with a wink. Hazel laughed, feeling lighter than she had in days. "I think we just lived the best one."

Marigold and Ember joined them, their lanterns glowing brightly in their paws. "This will be a story told for generations," Marigold said with a soft smile. "A story of how fear almost won—but hope was stronger."

Bramble fluttered down from his perch, plucking another **feather from his wing**. This one shimmered even brighter than the last, glowing with the soft light of a summer moon. He offered it to Hazel with a nod of respect. "For the one who kept the light alive," he murmured. "May you always carry it with you."

Hazel took the feather, feeling the warmth of its magic spread through her hand. **It wasn't just a gift—it was a reminder** that the magic of the Heart Oak would always be with them, as long as they believed in it.

Finn gave Hazel a playful nudge. "See? Told you we'd get a feather." Hazel laughed, slipping the feather into her pocket beside the charm. **This time, the weight in her heart was not fear—but joy.** The journey had been long and difficult, but they had made it through. **Together.**

As the burrowfolk sang beneath the lantern-lit branches, the Heart Oak stood tall and proud, its roots woven deep into the earth, its leaves whispering promises of new seasons to come. The shadows that had threatened the burrows were gone—**sealed not just by magic, but by trust, by love, and by the stories they shared.**

The night stretched on in celebration, with **laughter, music, and stories that would become legends**. And as the lanterns flickered softly above them, Hazel knew that the light they had kindled would never fade. "Let's go home, Hazy," Finn whispered, yawning as the first stars appeared in the sky. "We've got a story to tell."

Hazel smiled, her heart full. **The magic of the Heart Oak was safe.** And so was everything else that mattered—**hope, trust, and the light they had carried through the dark.**

Together, they made their way back through the winding burrows, **their lanterns glowing bright** against the night.

# A New Beginning

The morning arrived slowly, **soft sunlight filtering through the canopy**, dappling the burrow entrance with patches of gold. **The Heart Oak's branches shimmered**, its newly unfurled leaves whispering promises of spring. Hazel stood quietly beneath its roots, taking in the moment. The light felt different now—**not just warm, but steady**, as if the tree itself knew the worst was behind them.

Finn bounded up beside her, his face bright with excitement. "Think we'll ever see something this amazing again?" he asked, adjusting his scarf with a grin.

Hazel smiled, though a bittersweet knot curled in her chest. "I hope so." But she knew—deep down—that **this place would always be special**, no matter where they went from here. **The magic of the Heart Oak had become part of them.**

As the siblings prepared to leave, **the burrowfolk gathered beneath the great tree** one last time to offer their thanks. Each of them carried small gifts—**tokens of gratitude** for the journey Hazel and Finn had taken to save the Heart Oak.

Tumble Brewburrow handed Finn **a small bottle of enchanted ale**, the liquid inside sparkling like captured starlight. "For your next adventure," the badger said with a wink. "A drop of this, and you'll never lose your way."

Marigold Softpaw gave Hazel a **satchel filled with herbs**, tied with a ribbon of silver thread. "Yarrow for courage, moonflower petals for hope, and dreamroot for when you need to dream big," she whispered warmly.

Ember Quickpaw scampered forward, placing **a tiny book** into Finn's hands. "I wrote a poem just for you!" he squeaked proudly. "It's about brave heroes and lanterns that never go out."

Hazel and Finn exchanged smiles, their hearts full from the kindness of their friends. **These were no ordinary gifts—they were pieces of the burrowfolk's magic, memories to carry forward.**

Bramble the Owl swooped down from his perch, landing gracefully on a low branch. In his talons, he held **two small acorns**, their shells smooth and glimmering with soft, golden light.

"These," Bramble said, placing the acorns into Hazel and Finn's hands, "are seeds from the Heart Oak. They carry the tree's magic within them—**wherever you go, the magic will follow.** Plant them in a place that matters, and the magic will grow again."

Hazel stared at the small acorn in her hand, feeling its quiet hum. It was **a promise—a reminder** that even if they left the burrows, **the light would always be with them.** Finn tucked his acorn into his pocket, already dreaming of where he would plant it.

The burrowfolk gathered close, their lanterns glowing softly in the early light. **The shadows were gone**, but the bonds forged through their journey would remain—stronger than any fear.

Marigold's whiskers twitched as she gave Hazel a tight hug. "Don't be a stranger," she whispered. "You'll always have a place here."

Tumble grinned, clapping Finn on the back. "Next time you visit, there'll be a feast waiting!" he declared.

Bramble dipped his head, his amber eyes warm. "The magic of the Heart Oak is yours now," he murmured. "Carry it with you, and it will never fade."

With a final wave, Hazel and Finn turned toward the forest path, their **lanterns swinging gently** at their sides. The air smelled of **pine and damp earth**, alive with the promise of new adventures.

They walked in comfortable silence for a while, the soft hum of the burrows fading into the distance. Finn glanced at Hazel, a grin spreading across his face. "So, where do we plant our acorns?"

Hazel smiled as she twirled the **gleaming acorn** between her fingers. The weight of it felt comforting, not heavy, but grounding—like **holding a little piece of home** in her hand. "We'll know when we find the right place," she said softly, her voice carried on the cool morning breeze. "It'll feel just right, like it was meant to grow there."

Finn nodded, satisfied with her answer. He kicked a stone along the path, his lantern swinging at his side. **The forest around them seemed friendlier now**, as though the trees and roots that once whispered warnings now hummed a song of welcome and peace.

As they made their way back toward the edge of the forest, **small signs of magic danced along their path**.

Tiny **mushroom circles glowed softly** beneath the ferns, and a **pair of foxes trotted through the underbrush**, one of them playing a low, lilting tune on a reed flute. **Fireflies drifted lazily**, their lights flickering like distant stars, and somewhere far off, the faint sound of a stream babbled cheerfully over smooth stones.

Even the sky seemed to shimmer with possibility. **The forest was awake**, alive with the kind of quiet magic that only those who truly believe can see.

Finn grinned as a **squirrel darted past**, carrying a tiny pair of knitted mittens in its mouth. "Think Twig and Thistle sent us a parting gift?" he asked with a laugh.

Hazel chuckled. "Probably. I think half the burrow is going to keep finding ways to sneak little gifts into our pockets."

They stopped at the edge of the woods, where the trees parted to reveal the path that would take them back to **their grandmother's cottage.** For a moment, they stood in the shadow of the forest, **the ancient trees standing like guardians** between the world of the burrowfolk and the one waiting beyond.

Finn looked back toward the trees, his eyes bright with lingering wonder. "Do you think we'll ever find our way back?" he whispered, almost as if he were afraid to break the spell of the moment.

Hazel placed a hand on his shoulder, squeezing gently. "We will," she said. **"The burrows will always be there—just like the Heart Oak. And so will the magic."**

Finn pulled the tiny book of poetry from his pocket, flipping it open with a grin. "Good thing we've got Ember's book," he said. "It'll keep us ready for the next adventure."

Hazel smiled, and together, they continued down the path, **the forest fading gently behind them**, the lanterns swaying in time with their steps.

When they arrived at **their grandmother's cottage**, the old wooden porch greeted them with its familiar creaks and soft scent of herbs drying in the windows. The garden, overgrown with ivy and wildflowers, seemed **the perfect place for something magical to take root.**

Finn crouched down by the largest oak tree near the edge of the garden, digging a small hollow in the soft earth. Hazel knelt beside him, her acorn cradled carefully in her palm.

They planted their **two shimmering acorns** side by side, tucking them into the ground with care. **The earth hummed beneath their hands**, a quiet acknowledgment of the magic they had brought home.

Finn sat back on his heels, brushing dirt from his hands. "Do you think they'll grow fast?" he asked eagerly.

Hazel smiled, brushing a stray leaf from her hair. "Maybe not fast—but they'll grow strong." She touched the spot gently, **as if making a promise** to the small seeds they had planted. "They'll always have a little magic in them."

As they stood, a **soft breeze rustled the leaves above**, carrying the scent of pine and lavender. The wind seemed to murmur words just beyond hearing, as though **the Heart Oak itself was sending a message across the distance.**

Finn tilted his head, listening. "Did you hear that?"

Hazel closed her eyes, letting the breeze brush past her like an old friend. "I think it's saying... **thank you.**"

The breeze settled, leaving behind a sense of peace—a feeling that wherever life took them next, they would always carry **the magic of the burrows** with them.

As evening fell, Hazel and Finn sat together on the porch, their lanterns glowing softly between them. **The acorns they had planted hummed beneath the soil**, and though they couldn't see it yet, **something magical had already begun to take root.**

Finn yawned, stretching his arms over his head. "So... what do we call this story?" he asked sleepily.

Hazel leaned against the railing, the lantern light flickering gently in the twilight. **"The story of how two kids found magic underground,"** she said thoughtfully, "and learned that the light is strongest when it's shared."

Finn grinned. "Yeah. I like that." He held up the little poetry book with a laugh. "Think Ember will want us to send him a sequel?"

Hazel smiled, watching the stars slowly appear overhead. "I think... **this is just the beginning.**"

And as they sat together beneath the wide, open sky, with the lantern light glowing steadily between them, Hazel knew that no matter where they went, **they would always carry the light with them—a light that would never fade, no matter how dark the world became.**

The night stretched long and quiet, but **the magic they had found in the burrows lingered**—not in the air or the lanterns, but in their hearts, woven into every step they took, every story they told. The shadows would come and go, as they always did, but the light they carried would always be there—**a steady flame to guide them through the dark.**

And in the quiet garden beneath the old oak tree, **two tiny acorns stirred**, their roots stretching slowly toward the stars, ready to bloom with the magic of a new beginning.

This concludes the story of **Hazel and Finn's journey through the Burrowlands**. Though their time in the burrows has come to an end, **the magic lives on**—in every story told, every lantern lit, and every acorn planted. And no matter where their paths take them next, they will always know:

**The light is strongest when it is shared.**

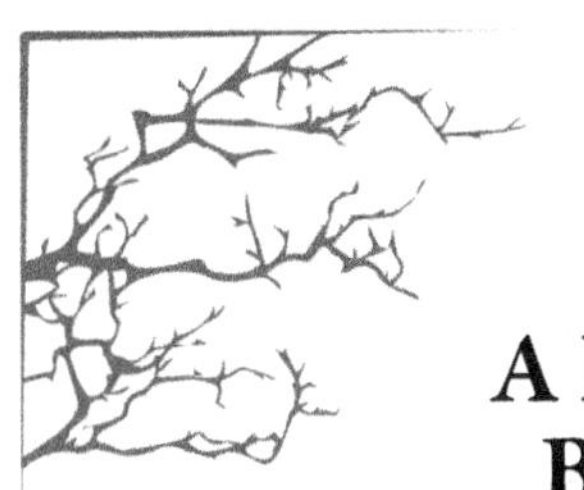

# A Poem of the Burrowfolk

Beneath the tangled forest floor,
Where roots entwine and tunnels soar,
Lies a world the daylight never sees—
A land of lanterns, moss, and leaves.
Softly hum the glowing streams,
Like silver threads that stitch through dreams.
Mushroom stools by fireside hearths,
Where songs and stories weave their sparks.
Here, life is stitched with gentle care—
Herbs hum lullabies through twilight air,
Petals glow beneath the moon's white gleam,
And burrowfolk drift through a starry dream.
The air smells sweet of cedar and rain,
Of elderflower, mint, and grain.
Foxes play flutes in shadowed glades,
While squirrels spin wool in cozy nooks made.
Rabbits plant seeds that whisper of spring,
And mice craft poems from everything—
A fallen leaf, a beetle's track,

The moonlight's kiss upon their back.
Their lanterns burn with steady grace,
Chasing fear from every space.
The burrows buzz with life so small,
Yet magic hums through roots and walls.
Here, time flows soft, like drifting snow,
And shadows come, but do not grow.
For light is shared in every word,
In every laugh and tale heard.
In autumn's dance, they spin with the leaves,
In winter's stillness, they sit and weave.
When springtime calls, they greet with song,
And through summer's warmth, they move along.
The burrowfolk teach what life will say:
**The smallest light can guide the way.**
For in each leaf and every root,
The world's great magic finds its truth.
So listen close, beneath the ground—
Where hums of quiet joy are found.
The lanterns glow, the acorns sprout,
And light within will never go out.

# Also by B. Humphrey

**Bigfoot Vs**
Bigfoot Vs Werewolves
Bigfoot Vs Vampires
Bigfoot Vs Aliens
Bigfoot Vs Yeti
Bigfoot Vs Werebear
Bigfoot Vs Mothman
Bigfoot Vs The Kandahar Giant
Bigfoot Vs Chimera
Bigfoot Vs Loch Ness Monster
Bigfoot Vs Wendigo
The Great Cryptid Wars
The Moon Curse Saga

**Retro Horrors: The Lost Decade**
Cassette Ghosts
Summer of the Black Star
The Arcade Incident
Dead End Drive – In

The Polaroid Project
Endless Paths: The Choose-Your-Own Doom Chronicles
Neon Dreams
The Forgotten Carnival
Satanic Panic
Skin of the Moon


**The Autumn Folklore Chronicles**
The Forest Of Forgotten Names
The Witch Of Windspindle Hollow
The Burrowfolk Chronicles


**The Fall Of America**
The Final Directive


**The Phantom Finders Club**
A Haunting On Maplewood Street
The Secrets Of Old Fort Tower
Ghosts OF The Infirmary


**The Starling Sleuths**
Detective Starling vol. 1
Detective Starling Vol. 2

**Winter Horrors**
Whispers of the Wendigo
Cold Cuts
The Dark Beneath


**Standalone**
The Witch of Blackwood Hollow
The Storied Mind
The Great Cryptid Wars
Sporefall